This book belongs to:

To our donor. Thank you for the awesome genes. —Christy

For my wonderful parents, who love and support me unfailingly. —Ciaee

~~

Zak's SAFARI

A Story about Donor-Conceived Kids of Two-Mom Families

By CHRISTY TYNER

Illustrated by CIAEE

Dear Reader,

Zak's Safari takes an honest, open, and age-appropriate approach to talking about donor conception and family diversity. Using a book like this one is an excellent way to begin (or continue) conversations with children about their origins, or to educate child friends or relatives about your family. To help with your discussions I offer these 4 tips for talking to kids about donor conception.

1) Keep it simple.

Especially for young children, simple, honest and personal is best. Make the story one about love and connection. For example, you might say, "Mama and I wanted a child. It takes an egg from a woman and a sperm from a man to make a baby. Your Mama provided the egg and a man called a donor provided the sperm. You grew in Mama's body and when you were born, I held you and changed your diapers. Your Mama and I are your parents, we love you, and we take care of you." Remember, whatever complex emotions you may have about the conception journey, for your child the story of how they came to be is happy, magical, and full of love.

2) Tell early.

Telling early has many advantages. First, it gives the parent(s) the opportunity to get comfortable with the topic and try out different ways of telling the family story. Some parents practice by telling the story to their infant, to each other, to a partner, or to a friend. Second, sharing early normalizes the topic, so children who learn early know they can go to their parents when they have questions. Lastly, early disclosure ensures that children learn this important information from their parents—and not from others who may have less positive or less informed views on donor conception.

3) Tell often.

Thinking of disclosure as a process, rather than a one-time event, frees parents from having to explain every aspect at once. Most children will have different questions and interests at different ages. As your child evolves their understanding, you can evolve your explanations by answering their questions as they come up. Finding ways to keep the dialogue going (such as creating a family book or having books like Zak's Safari on the bookshelf) will remind your child that this is an acceptable topic to talk about.

4) Differentiate between people who make you and people who take care of you.

Children often want to know that they, like everyone else on the planet, came from two people and are often understandably curious about the donor. The fact that the donor is a person (not just some disembodied cells or genes) is important. However, it is also important to clarify that the donor is not a parent. For example, you could say, "There are people who help make you (like Mama and the donor) and there are people who take care of you (like Mom and Mama). Sometimes these people are the same (Mama) and sometimes they are different (Mom and the donor). The people who take care of you (Mama and Mom) are your parents."

I have spoken to parents who feel that this places too much emphasis on the donor. They want to focus only on the people who are in the child's life, not on someone the child doesn't know. We have found in our research that the donor is often important to donor-conceived children. This doesn't diminish their love for their parent(s). Curiosity about the donor is common and normal and is likely to vary from age to age and from child to child.

Many parents are nervous about talking with children about conception. Talking with our kids about their origins is not that different from teaching them about other complex aspects of their lives. As donor-conceived families, this is part of the journey of parenthood for us, and part of growing up for our kids.

You can do it!

Alice Ruby, MPH, Executive Director, The Sperm Bank of California, and Mama through donor conception

Hello! Welcome to Zak's breathtaking, rip-roaring, electrifying, mind-blowing, heart-pounding adventure tours!

Today

we'll be heading out in my custom-built swamp-jeep to witness the hatching of a rare baby albino alligator in the wild. Be sure to hold on tight, everybody, because this is going to be the ride of your life!

I'm **Zak**,

and I'll be
your guide
on this

fine,

warm,

sunny

day.

Never fear!

A good tour guide
is *always* ready

with a rainy-day
backup plan.

Ah-ha!

Well, I don't usually do this, but – *just this once* – I invite you to join me on a very special, incredibly rare tour of...

my family!

Right this way, folks.
Let's start from the
beginning, shall we?

Once upon a time my parents met,

fell in love,

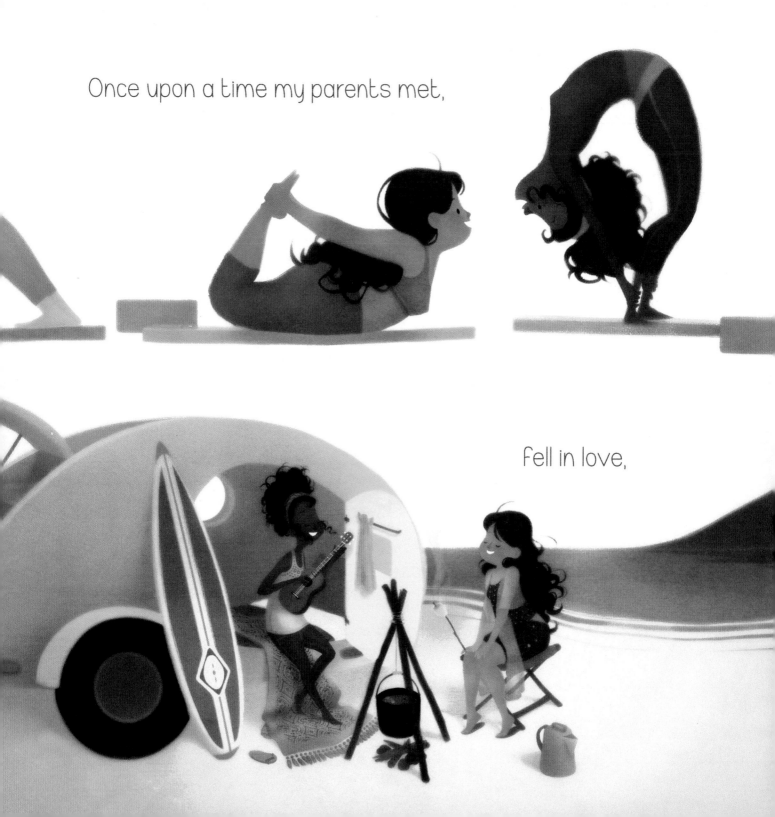

and wanted *more than anything* to have a baby.

So they decided to make one.

Now,

as you super smart tourists may already know, there are two things you need to make a baby. Can anyone tell me what these are?

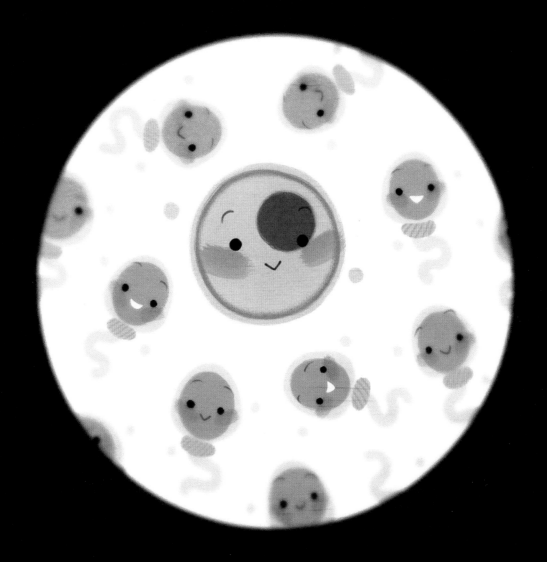

That's right: an **egg** and a **sperm**! Most women's bodies make eggs and most men's bodies make sperm. Eggs and sperm are so small you can only see them under a microscope. Here, take a look.

There are *many* different types of families.

Some families have
a mom and **a dad**,
so they already
have the sperm and
egg that they need
to make a baby.

Some families have
one or **two dads.**
Since they already
have the sperm,
they just need the
egg. They might ask
a friend for her help
to make their baby.

Some families have **one** or **two moms.** They already have the egg, so they need the sperm. One way to get sperm is to ask a special friend to give them some of his.

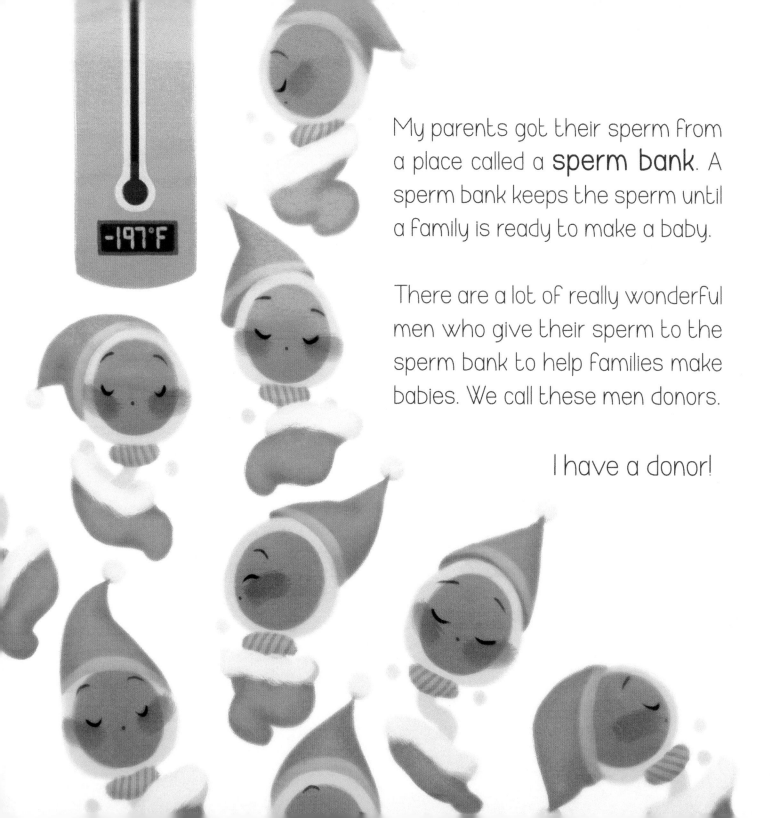

My parents got their sperm from a place called a **sperm bank**. A sperm bank keeps the sperm until a family is ready to make a baby.

There are a lot of really wonderful men who give their sperm to the sperm bank to help families make babies. We call these men donors.

I have a donor!

-197°F

This is Alice. She works at the sperm bank.

Alice helped my parents look through a book to decide
which donor's sperm to use. There were lots of donors
for my parents to choose from.

Sperm and eggs are amazing! Did you know that they carry secret instructions that tell a baby what to look like? It's true! You get half of who you are from the sperm and half from the egg.

For example, if the donor has **brown eyes**, his sperm carries instructions that might make a baby with **brown eyes**.

If the mother has **red, curly hair**, her child might have **red, curly hair**.

If the donor is **tall**, the baby might grow up to be **tall**. These secret instructions are called genes.

I know my parents chose an awesome donor, 'cause I'm pretty sure I got some of his awesome genes.

Anyway, my parents got the sperm that they needed to make me. They put it inside my mom's body, where it swam and swam with its strong tail until it found the egg that was waiting inside of her.

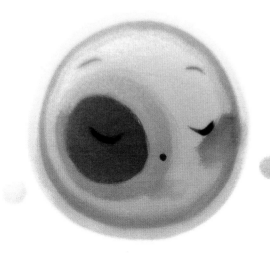

The sperm and the egg cuddled up so close together that they became one thing. And this one thing was the beginning of me.

If you can believe it, I was even smaller than a grain of sand back then. But I grew strong and healthy inside my mom's warm, safe body. When it was time, **I was born.**

My parents were so excited to finally meet me! They held me in their arms and sang me sweet songs and told me how much they loved me. They protected me and rocked me to sleep and fed me. They played with me and showed me the world and taught me everything.

My parents love me so much that it makes my heart feel like breakdancing.

And *that*...

is how we became a **family**.

We're just like every family, everywhere.

We eat our meals together

and we play together.

We have parties with friends

and we hang out with family.

We have picnics at the beach,

go for long nature hikes,

and have adventures
in the snow.

We sometimes argue,

but we **always** make up.

My parents tell me
 that when I was born
the adventure truly began.
And it hasn't stopped since.
This is the breathtaking, rip-roaring,
electrifying, mind-blowing, heart-pounding
adventure of family.

Be sure to hold on tight to everybody, because this...

is the
ride
of
your
life.

CHRISTY lives in the San Francisco Bay Area with her wife and two children. When not riding the roller coaster of family life, she loves imagining new children's books. Her first book, *Mama Midwife: A Birth Adventure*, was self-published in 2013.

CIAEE *(pronounced: ji-AH-yee)* is a Malaysian-born illustrator who currently resides in San Francisco with her dear husband, Tom. She delights in making things with her hands, and finds great joy in telling stories through her pictures.

Our Story

Made in the USA
Monee, IL
08 March 2021